RAISEL'S

To Beverly, for planting the seed —E.S.　　　*For Sharon* —S.G.

PURIM IS THE JEWISH HOLIDAY that celebrates the story of Esther, the Jewish queen of Persia. Esther is beloved
for having saved her people from destruction at the hand of Haman, the king's wicked adviser. Her story appears in the Bible
and is called *Megillat Esther*, the Scroll of Esther. On Purim, Jews wearing the costumes of the characters reenact the story at joyous parties.

Farrar Straus Giroux Books for Young Readers • An imprint of Macmillan Publishing Group, LLC
120 Broadway, New York, NY 10271 • mackids.com

Text copyright © 1999 by Erica Silverman. Illustrations copyright © 1999 by Susan Gaber
All rights reserved. Printed in China by RR Donnelley Asia Printing Solutions Ltd., Dongguan City, Guangdong Province.
Color separations by Hong Kong Scanner Arts. Designed by Filomena Tuosto
First edition, 1999
12 11 10 9 8 7 6 5 4

Library of Congress Cataloging-in-Publication Data
Silverman, Erica.
    Raisel's riddle / Erica Silverman ; pictures by Susan Gaber. — 1st ed.
        p.   cm.
    Summary: A Jewish version of the Cinderella story, in which a poor but educated young woman captivates her "Prince Charming," a rabbi's son, at a Purim ball.
    ISBN 978-0-374-36168-1
    [1. Fairy tales. 2. Jews—Folklore.] I. Gaber, Susan, ill.   II. Cinderella. English.   III. Title.
    PZ8.S3457Rai   1999
    398.2'089924—DC21   97-29421
    ISBN 978-0-374-46200-0 (PJ Library edition)   Code 0222/B570/A7

RIDDLE

STORY BY ERICA SILVERMAN

PICTURES BY SUSAN GABER

FARRAR, STRAUS AND GIROUX

ONCE UPON A TIME in a village in
Poland there lived an orphan girl named
Raisel. She was raised by her grandfather,
a poor scholar who studied day and night.

Because of his vast learning, the villagers
turned to him for wisdom and guidance.
They paid him when they could with cheese
or bread or wood for the fire. In this way,
Raisel and her grandfather got by.

One day, Raisel sat by her grandfather's side, watching as he pored over a thick book. "Zaydeh," she asked, "why do you study all the time?"

"Why, indeed?" He looked at her with twinkling eyes. "It is written that learning is more precious than rubies, more lasting than gold. Rubies may be lost and gold stolen, but that which you learn is yours forever."

"Zaydeh," said Raisel, "I want to study, too."

Raisel's grandfather began to teach her. Every day, they read and recited from the ancient texts, often late into the night.

Then came a harsh winter. Raisel's grandfather fell ill. On a bitter cold night, as she sat reading to him, he breathed his last breath.

The villagers visited Raisel with words of comfort. They brought what little food they could spare.

But Raisel did not want to become a burden to them. As the snow began to melt, she set out to seek work. Wearing a tattered shawl, she followed a dirt path through forest and field, until at last she reached the gates of the city. She made her way through crooked, narrow streets. She stopped at every house to ask for work. Again and again, she was turned away.

Beyond the synagogue, Raisel entered a courtyard and knocked on a door.

A woman in an apron opened it. "The poorhouse is down the street," the woman said gruffly.

"I am seeking work," Raisel explained. "I can cook and clean."

The woman turned up her nose. "This is the fine home of a most distinguished rabbi. I am his cook, the best in all of Poland, and I manage the household, too."

At that moment, the rabbi came to the door.

"Please," Raisel begged, "I am strong and capable. For a place to sleep and some bread, I will work very hard."

The rabbi turned to the cook. "Surely you could use some help."

Scowling, the cook led Raisel to the kitchen. "You might be capable, rag girl, but that doesn't mean you can push your way into my home and steal my job!" She pointed to a large washtub. "Fill it to the top. And be quick!"

Raisel hurried back and forth, hauling bucket after bucket from the well to the washtub until finally it was full.

"Not fast enough!" The cook kicked it over. "Do it again."

Later that night, the cook showed Raisel to a bed of straw behind the oven. Early the next morning, she shook Raisel from her sleep. "Scrub the hearth until it sparkles!" she ordered.

And so the days passed. From sunup to sundown, Raisel held her tongue, hid her tears, and did as she was told.

As the holiday of Purim drew near, Raisel worked harder than ever. There were costumes to make ready, a feast to prepare.

On Purim morning, Raisel walked across the courtyard, struggling with a heavy bundle of wood. She bumped into someone. Logs fell, and quickly she bent down to pick them up.

"I'm so sorry," said a kind voice. "Silly of me to read and walk at the same time."

Raisel looked up.

It was the rabbi's son. He helped her gather the wood and carry it to the kitchen. Then he walked on, his nose back in his book.

The cook's eyes blazed. "I saw you talking sweetly to the rabbi's son, trying to win favor in the household. From now on, keep to yourself or things will go badly for you."

That afternoon, guests dressed in their Purim costumes sat down to a fine feast of beet soup, roast duck, potato pancakes, and noodle pudding. Raisel cleared the table, listening to the young women entertain the rabbi's son with riddles.

"What has a face but no mouth?" asked one.

"A clock," said the rabbi's son.

"I have a good riddle," said another.

Raisel lingered, wanting to hear more.

The rabbi's son saw her. "Do you have a riddle, too?" He smiled.

The cook pushed Raisel into the kitchen. "If you cannot stay out of sight," she warned, "I will lock you in the pantry."

After dinner, the rabbi and his guests climbed into horse-drawn wagons and rode off to see the Purim play.

Raisel sighed. "I wish I could go, too."

"In your costume of rags?" The cook sneered. "Take your dinner from what is left over. Then get to work." She pointed at the piles of plates and pots and pans waiting to be washed.

Raisel carried her meager meal outside and sat by the well.

An old beggar woman hobbled toward her.

"I can see that you are hungry," Raisel said. She offered the woman her own plate of food.

The old woman ate. Then she reached for Raisel's hands. "Because of your kind heart, I grant you three wishes." She leaned closer. "But know this—magic does not last past midnight."

Magic? Was it possible? Could she go to the Purim play? Raisel shut her eyes. "I wish . . . I wish for a Purim costume."

Suddenly she felt different. Opening her eyes, she gasped. "I am dressed as Queen Esther!" She twirled around and around.

Again, she shut her eyes. "I wish for a horse-drawn wagon."

A wagon stood waiting! Trembling with excitement, she climbed in.

Raisel entered the hall. Everyone's eyes turned toward her.

"What a beautiful costume," whispered one person.

"I wonder who she is," whispered another.

After the Purim play, a klezmer band made music. The rabbi's son came up to Raisel and introduced himself. "Forgive my boldness," he said, "but in that costume you are the loveliest Queen Esther here. It is a pity there are no prizes tonight."

Raisel blushed. "It is only a costume. As it is written, 'Look not at the flask but at what it contains.'"

The rabbi's son stared in surprise. "How is it that you know words from the Talmud?"

Raisel's eyes grew moist. "My zaydeh, blessed be his memory, was a devout scholar."

"Have I heard of him?" asked the rabbi's son.

"It is not likely," replied Raisel. "He lived in a small village far from here."

"And where do you live?"

Raisel was silent. He did not realize that she was the rag girl in his kitchen. Quickly, she changed the subject. "May I tell you a riddle?" Before he could reply, she made one up.

"*What's more precious than rubies, more lasting*
 than gold?
What can never be traded, stolen, or sold?
What comes with great effort and takes time,
 but then—
Once yours, will serve you again and again?"

All at once, a clock began to chime midnight. Bong! Bong!

"I must go!" Raisel raced across the hall.

"Wait!" called the rabbi's son.

Bong! Bong! She ran through the doors.

Bong! She climbed into the wagon.

Bong! She grabbed the reins. The horse took off.

Bong! Bong! The wagon clattered down cobblestone streets.

Bong! Bong! At last, it stopped at the rabbi's house.

Raisel hurried to the kitchen. Bong! "Oh no! The dishes!" She closed her eyes. "I wish the kitchen spotless!"

Bong! The kitchen was clean. And Raisel was back in her old rags. Sadly, she curled up on her bed of straw. She hardly slept, thinking of her conversation with the rabbi's son.

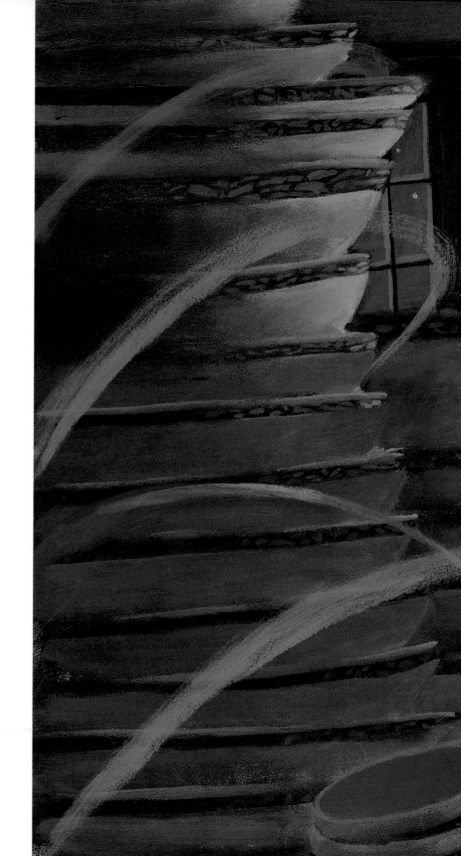

The next morning, as Raisel was working in the kitchen, she heard voices outside. "Are we having company?" she asked the cook.

"We, indeed! I warned you to keep to yourself!" The cook pushed Raisel into the pantry and barred the door.

It was dark but for one ray of light. Raisel climbed on a stool and followed the light to a hole in the door. Peering through it, she could see all the way to the dining room, where guests had gathered.

"Welcome, friends, and thank you for coming," the rabbi said. "Last night a girl told my son a riddle that showed rare intelligence. This is the girl my son wants to marry. She must be found."

"I told him a wonderful riddle," said a woman in a fancy hat.

"Come hear my rhyme. Now what is that
Over my head but under my hat?"

The rabbi's son shook his head. "The answer is hair," he said. "But that is not the right riddle."

More young women came forward.

The rabbi's son listened to one riddle after another. Finally, he sighed. "These riddles are common. The one I seek spoke of something precious and lasting."

Raisel's heart fluttered. Could it be hers? She banged on the door with all her might.

The rabbi's son hurried into the kitchen. "What was that noise?"

The cook shrugged. "Just the rag girl. She's cleaning the pantry."

"My name is Raisel. I, too, told you a riddle," called Raisel through the door.

The cook scoffed. "She was here all night, washing dishes."

"I would hear her riddle," said the rabbi's son. He unbarred the door.

Raisel stepped forward.

"What's more precious than rubies, more lasting
    than gold?

What can never be traded, stolen, or sold?"

"That is it!" cried the rabbi's son. He
completed the riddle.

"What comes with great effort and takes time,
    but then—

Once yours, will serve you again and again?"

He took her hand. "Will you marry me?"

"Only if you can answer my riddle," replied
Raisel.

He smiled. "The answer is learning."

"Yes!" said Raisel. "Yes!"

And so Raisel and the rabbi's son were
married. They lived and learned happily ever
after.